Treasury

By Sheila Sweeny Higginson
Illustrated by the Disney Storybook Artists

DISNEY PRESS

NEW YORK

ISBN 978-1-4231-3110-6

Printed in China

Contents

Minnie's Rainbow

By Sheila Sweeny Higginson

Illustrated by Loter, Inc.

Disney PRESS
NEW YORK

Minnie has just finished reading a book.
She's asked all her friends to come take a look.

She learned about something you see in the sky.
A colorful arc that the birds fly right by.

But what makes a rainbow that follows the rain?
Let's find out as Minnie and her friends explain.

Red, orange, and yellow are one, two, and three.
Green is four. Blue is five. Violet is six, as you can see.

But there's more to each rainbow you see in the sky.
A whole spectrum of colors, so let's find out why!

A rainbow is made of the colors of light.
When we look at it whole, we can see only white.

But when white light is split, then more colors appear.
If you tried counting them, it might take a whole year!

There are not only colors like red, green, and blue.
There are some you can't see with your eyes. Yes, it's true!

So what makes a rainbow? What is it we see?
All the waves that are part of the light, naturally!

You can make a rainbow right on your wall! What colors do you see?

You need:
- A small mirror
- A clear jar filled with water
- A flashlight
- A white wall

How it works:
1. Place the mirror inside the jar.
2. Bring the jar into a dark room with white walls.
3. Turn on the flashlight and shine the light onto the mirror.
4. If you don't see a rainbow, try changing the angle of the flashlight until you do.

UP, UP, AND AWAY!

AN ADVENTURE IN SHADOWS AND SHAPES
By Sheila Sweeny Higginson
Illustrated by the Disney Storybook Artists

DISNEY PRESS
NEW YORK

Donald and his friends were standing outside the Clubhouse on a crisp, bright day.

"Oh, Donald," Daisy said, "look at the sky! It's lovely!"

"Shhh!" Donald whispered. "Don't make a move! Something is following me and I'm going to find out who, or what, it is!"

Daisy giggled as she looked behind Donald. "Oh, my!" said Daisy. "There *is* something following you! It's wearing a sailor's cap—just like yours. It's got cute webbed feet—just like yours. And when you move, it moves, too."

"Aw, phooey," Donald quacked as he turned around and saw his shadow. "That is a fine-looking shape, but I still don't trust it!"

The friends laughed at Donald as he glared at his shadow.

"Cheer up, buddy," Mickey said. "Why don't you leave your shadow on the ground and come with me?"

"I don't know," Donald said moping. "Where are we going?"

"Up, up, and away!" Mickey cheered. "Who wants to help Minnie and me fly our hot-air balloon?"

"I sure do!" shouted Goofy.

"You can count me out," Donald grumbled.

"I don't trust that thing. Besides," he added, "I'm not missing lunch."

"Aw, come on, Donald," Minnie pleaded. "I've packed a square meal for each of us. Up, up, and away!"

"Something's wrong," Mickey said. "The balloon won't fill with air!"

"That's too bad, buddy," said Donald, trying to hide a grin. "I guess we'll just have to go back to the Clubhouse for lunch."

"Oh, Toodles!" Mickey said. "Do we have a Mousketool that can help?" Toodles appeared. "Do any of you know how we can use this tool?" Mickey asked.

"I know, Mickey!" answered Minnie. "We can turn the crank to inflate the balloon with hot air."

"Why, you're right, Minnie!" Mickey shouted.

"We've got ears! Say cheers!"

Soon, the friends were floating high above the Clubhouse.
"Up, up, and away!" cried Daisy. "This is fun!"

"Look, everyone!" yelled Minnie. "Can you see the Clubhouse from here? It looks so small! And there are so many shapes below us. I see a heart, a triangle, and a rectangle. What do you see?"

"I see a triangle, too!" Mickey shouted. "And there are Chip and Dale playing a round of golf!"

"It should be called a triangle of golf," laughed Daisy. "Just look at all those triangle-shaped flags!"

"What's a triangle?" asked Goofy as he bit into his sandwich.

"A triangle is a shape with three sides that have points at the ends—sort of like your sandwich," Minnie explained.

"Or like that?" Goofy questioned, as he pointed to a huge triangle in front of the balloon.

It was the top of a mountain! Suddenly, a gust of wind whisked the friends right toward it!

"We need help," cried Mickey. "Oh, Toodles!"

Toodles appeared with a triangle, a patch, a ladder, and a telescope.

"Which tool should we use?" asked Minnie.

"All of them!" said Mickey. "Daisy, ring the triangle for help!"

Daisy rang the triangle, but it didn't help them get off the mountain.

"Minnie, patch the hole!"

Minnie put a square patch on the round hole in the balloon, but it was too small.

"Goofy, look through the telescope!" Goofy held the telescope and saw that the ground looked very far away.

"There's only one tool left," yelled Mickey. "To the ladder!"

Mickey dropped the ladder over the side of the balloon. "We've got ears! Say cheers!" said Mickey. "If we can't get the balloon to go back up, then we'll have to go down—one step at a time."

"Me first! Me first!" shouted Donald.

"We're going to do this fair and square," Mickey announced.

"Take a piece of paper with a number on it. Whoever gets number one goes first. Whoever gets number two goes second. Get the idea?"

The friends headed down the ladder one by one. Everyone was happy to be standing on firm ground again.

"We're in great shape, unlike our balloon," said Mickey. "But we're going to have to hike back home. It's not far —just down that path . . . or maybe it's that one."

The friends trudged along, growing more and more tired. "I think we've been walking in circles," Mickey finally said. "I'm sure I've seen this tree before."

"Oh, Toodles!" Toodles appeared, showing three pictures of Mickey. Mickey shared them with his friends.

"I'm standing in front of the Clubhouse, and my shadow is different in each picture. In the morning, my shadow falls in front of me. At noon, I have no shadow. In the evening, my shadow falls behind me. Do any of you know what this could mean?"

The friends studied the pictures carefully.

"I've got it!" Donald shouted. "Right now, it's late and the sun is setting behind us. Toodles shows us that in the evening, our shadows point toward the Clubhouse. If we follow them, they'll lead us back home."

Donald was correct. The shadows helped the friends head in the right direction. Soon, they arrived back at the Clubhouse. Everyone was hungry from the long trip.

"Well, Donald," Daisy said, "do you trust your shadow now?"

"I'll trust the handsome guy to lead me home," Donald answered. "But he'd better not ask me to share my pie!"

Parents Page

Learning the names of shapes is an important skill for preschoolers. You can help your child master the vocabulary of shapes and the spatial concepts associated with them by playing simple games throughout the day.

1. LEAD A SHAPES SEARCH. Let your child choose a shape and, as you go about your day, have him or her identify all the circles, squares, rectangles, or triangles that can be found at home or in the neighborhood.

2. FIND THE RIGHT WORDS. Help your child learn the names of less-common shapes, such as hearts, diamonds, and ovals.

3. MAKE SHAPES. Cut out shapes from cardboard or thick paper. Make a "shapes mobile" to hang in your child's room. Cut a piece of paper into a square, then fold it corner to corner to make a triangle. Put two squares together end-to-end to make a rectangle. Draw shapes on the ground or in sand, using a stick or shovel. Make foods in different shapes. For example, use cookie cutters to make fun-shaped biscuits or sandwiches.

4. TALK ABOUT THE PHYSICS OF SHAPES. Why does a ball need to be round? Why are steps squared off? Why are most pebbles and rocks roundish in shape? Why are most books rectangles or squares?

5. PLAY NAME GAMES. What words can your child name that include the word "round" (around, surround)? What words rhyme with "square" (bear, care, chair, dare, fair, glare, hare/hair, mare, pear/pair, rare, stare/stair, tear, there/their, wear/where)? "Round" (bound, clowned, found, ground, hound, pound, sound, wound)? How many words start with "tri-" (triangle, tricycle, triplet)?

6. PLAY SHADOW GAMES. Have fun with your child—create various shadow shapes on the wall at home or on the ground outdoors. Play shadow tag, in which each player tries to step on the other players' shadows.

LOOK BEFORE YOU LEAP!

By Sheila Sweeny Higginson
Illustrated by the Disney Storybook Artists

Mickey and Goofy were enjoying a quiet game of chess. Just as Mickey was about to make a move, something soared through the window and landed right in the middle of the chessboard.

"What was that?" Mickey asked.

The two friends looked carefully at something that looked right back at them. It was green. It had webbed feet. It said, "Ribbit, ribbit."

It was a frog—a very jumpy frog. Goofy tried to grab it. **PLOP!** The frog leaped out of Goofy's hands and right onto the silly switch. The room began to spin around. Mickey tried to grab the frog, but it leaped right toward the . . .

. . . kitchen sink. **KERPLUNK!**

"You really should look before you leap!" Mickey said to the frog.

"What are we going to do about this big puddle?" Goofy asked.

"Oh, Toodles!" Mickey called. "We need some Mouseketools—right now!"

"The mop is the right tool for this job," said Mickey. "Thanks, Toodles!"

All of Mickey's hard work made Goofy hungry. He decided to make lunch. Just then, the frog took a giant leap right toward . . .

. . . Goofy's sandwich. **SQUISH!**

"Stop!" Mickey cried as Goofy was about to take
a bite.

"You really should look before you leap," Goofy said to
the frog. "And I should look before I bite!"

Goofy carried the frog outside.

"Hold on tight," Mickey said. "He's pretty slippery."

"I have him . . . I have him . . . **OOPS!** I don't have him!"

Goofy yelped as the frog leaped right toward . . .

. . . Daisy's painting! **SPLAT!**

"You should look before you leap!" Daisy said as the paint splattered everywhere. "Now my painting—and my clothes—are a mess."

"Hey, there, little friend," Mickey said to the frog. "Slow down!"

But it was too late. The frog leaped out from behind Daisy's painting and headed straight toward . . .

. . . Mickey's bicycle. **BOING!** He zoomed down the road, holding tightly to the handlebars. He was heading straight for a cliff.

"Oh, no!" Goofy shouted.

"Oh, Toodles!" yelled Mickey. "We need you!"

"The lasso is the right tool for this job," said Mickey. "Thanks, Toodles!"

Mickey and Goofy carefully pulled the bicycle back from the edge of the cliff.

"I think we should help our friend the frog find a nice, safe pond," Mickey said. "Then he can leap without causing any trouble."

The frog jumped up and down in agreement. Then he hopped away down the road with Mickey and Goofy following behind him.

The frog stopped hopping right in front of the pizzeria.
Slowly, Mickey and Goofy crept up behind him.

"We've got to get him before he leaps!" Mickey whispered.
But it was too late. Just as Mickey reached for him, the
frog leaped right onto a . . .

. . . pizza. **SLOSH!**

"You should look before you leap!" shouted the man behind the counter as tomato sauce dripped off the pizza.

The frog stopped for a moment to lick himself off. Then he hopped down Main Street, heading right toward Minnie and Pluto.

"Maybe Minnie and Pluto can help us catch our frog friend and take him to a nice pond," Mickey shouted.
  But the frog had other ideas. He took a great big leap and landed right inside . . .

. . . the goldfish bowl. **SPLASH!** The big wave made the goldfish fly right out. Minnie gently put the goldfish back into its bowl.

"I don't know if we'll ever find a pond for froggie. We need some help!" Goofy sighed.

"Oh, Toodles!" Mickey called.

"The net is the right tool for this job," said Mickey. At last, they held the frog safely in the net.

"He seems sad," Goofy said.

"I think you're right, Goofy," Mickey agreed. Then he looked up ahead and saw something that made him, and the frog, smile.

"I think we've found just the right place for you, froggie," Mickey said.

The friends walked quickly down the street toward the fountain. Carefully, Mickey placed the net on the ground and began to lift the frog out. But the frog was impatient.
Out he hopped, heading straight for the . . .

... fountain. He landed with a
SWOOSH! right next to another frog.

"Ribbit, ribbit," he said.

"Ribbit, ribbit," she replied.

"Maybe we didn't find a pond," said Mickey, "but we did find a good place for him to splash and leap."

"We've also found the frog a friend," noticed Minnie. "And they look very happy to see each other!"

"I think Minnie's goldfish is happy, *too*!" added Goofy.

Later, while Donald, Minnie, and Daisy made dinner,
Mickey and Goofy got back to their game of chess.

"C'mon, Mickey," Goofy said, "you haven't made a move in a long time."

"I know, I know," replied Mickey. "I just want to make sure I look carefully before I leap!"

QUICK QUIZ

Try this quiz to see how much of the story you can remember! Read the sentences and decide if each one is true. If it is, put a tick in the ✔ box. If it is false, put a cross in the ✘ box.

1 Mickey and Goofy are playing a game of snakes and ladders.

☐ ☐
✔ ✘

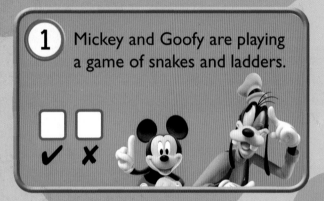

2 The frog leaps onto the silly switch.

☐ ☐
✔ ✘

3 Goofy makes a hamburger for his lunch.

☐ ☐
✔ ✘

4 The frog leaps onto Donald's painting.

☐ ☐
✔ ✘